NO PLACE LIKE HOME

No Place Like Home

BY

HESBA STRETTON

THE AUTHOR OF "JESSICA'S FIRST PRAYER," AND "LITTLE
MEG'S CHILDREN."

CURIOSMITH

MINNEAPOLIS

Published by Curiosmith.
P. O. Box 390293, Minneapolis, Minnesota, 55439.
Internet: curiosmith.com.
E-mail: shopkeeper@curiosmith.com.

Previously published by THE RELIGIOUS TRACT SOCIETY in 1881.

Definitions are from *Webster's Revised Unabridged Dictionary,* 1828 and 1913.

Scripture verses are from *The Holy Bible*, King James Version.

ISBN 9781935626855

CONTENTS

Chapter 1

AN OLD HOVEL

There was not another home like it in all the parish of Broadmoor. It was a half-ruined hut, with walls bulging outwards, and a ragged roof of old thatch, overgrown with moss and yellow stonecrop. A rusty iron pipe in one corner served as a chimney to the flat hearth, which was the only fireplace within; and a very small lattice window of greenish glass, with a bull's eye in each pane, let in but little of the summer sunshine, and hardly a gleam of the winter's gloomy light. Only a few yards off, the hut could not be distinguished from the ruins of an old limekiln, near which it had been built to shelter the lime-burners during their intervals of work. There was but one room downstairs, with an earthen floor trodden hard by the trampling of heavy feet, whilst under the thatch there was a little loft, reached by a steep ladder and a square hole in the ceiling, where the roof came down on each side to the rough flooring, and nowhere was there height enough for even a short person to stand upright.

The furniture was as rude and simple as the home itself. The good household chattels,[1] on which Ruth Medway had prided herself when she lived in her pretty cottage in the village street,

1 Chattel—any item of movable or immovable property.

had never come to this poor hovel. There was a broken chair or two, a table-top propped upon an unbarked trunk of a young fir tree from the woods behind the limekiln, a little cracked crockery, two or three old boxes, and the indispensable saucepan and kettle in which she did all her cooking. Upstairs was a low pallet bedstead with a flock-bed, and, on the floor beside it, a mattress stuffed with chaff, close under the roof, where the thatch must almost have touched the sleeper's face. There was no window into this loft; the only light came through the square hole in the floor.

"Home is home, be it never so homely;" and Ruth Medway had learned to love the quiet place where her youngest and her dearest child had been born. Behind the house lay the Limekiln Woods, once a busy place of quarries and kilns, but left long ago to the growth of trees and brushwood—the haunt of all kinds of wild woodland creatures, hollow with rabbit-burrows, and thickly peopled with singing birds, and with the game that the squire loved to preserve. Excepting in the shooting season, when the sharp crack of guns was to be heard all day long, there was no noise to drown the buzz of the humble-bee, and the low whirring of the unseen grasshopper, and the hundred faint and delicate sounds which fill the stillness of an unfrequented green wood. Day and night, summer and winter, had their special signs and sounds there, all well known to Ishmael, the youngest son of old Humphrey Medway.

He was the youngest son, and the most unwelcome to his father. Humphrey had given but a scanty welcome to his first-born child, and each successor had been received with growing surliness. Ishmael came the last, when his mother's hair was already grey and her back bent with hard toil at outdoor labor. The eldest son was grown up and married, and the little love he might have once felt for his mother had hardened into indifference, whilst the other children, those who were living, were scattered abroad, seldom caring to return home. Humphrey never mentioned any of them; but sometimes of an evening, when Ruth rested for a little while, and sat watching the kettle boil on the crackling fire of sticks, she would count their names over on her fingers—eight names over which she sighed, but at the ninth her brown wrinkled face wore a fleeting smile as she muttered, "Ishmael."

On the whole, Ruth was not given to brooding over the past; for she lived too hard a life to keep her memory green. She had grown fond of this lonely hut, where Ishmael had been born; and he had never known any other home. There was nothing in it to prevent him keeping pet dormice, and hedgehogs found in the hollows of the wood; though the gamekeeper would not let him have a rabbit, or allow Ruth to keep a cat; and a dog was not to be thought of. But a tame starling, and the white owl which had chosen its roost under their thatch, and answered his call in the dusk, swooping noiselessly through the air, made the place full of life and interest to him. All the woods behind had been his playground from his earliest childhood; and not the finest house in Broadmoor could have tempted Ishmael to exchange his home for it.

Ruth had taught herself to read after she was married; when Humphrey soon began to leave her alone in the evening, and kept her sitting up late for his return from the village inn. Her loneliness had led her to reading the Bible—the only book she possessed beside a Prayer-Book and an old collection of hymns. She had learned to believe quite simply, with no doubt in her inmost heart, that "God so loved the world, that He gave His only begotten Son, that whosoever believeth in Him should not perish, but have everlasting life;"[1] and that Jesus Christ had really

1 John 3:16.

"given His life as a ransom"[1] for her. With these two thoughts firmly rooted in her mind, she read the Bible eagerly; and it was from its old well-worn pages she had chosen the name of her youngest and dearest child: "Ishmael; because the Lord hath heard thy affliction."[2]

Ruth had never been a woman of many words; and she was very silent about those things which were deepest in her heart. Humphrey was accustomed to boast himself of her subjection to him, as not daring to "cheep"[3] a word against him. In her young days she had been one of the village choir; and now Ishmael sat in the singing gallery in her old place. It was one of her greatest pleasures to creep just within the church door, where her poor clothing would be least noticed, and listen to the voices in the gallery overhead, and to join in singing "Glory be to the Father" at the close of each familiar psalm. There her bent back seemed to ache less, and her wearied limbs felt rested. Often in the week, as she picked stones or hoed thistles in the fields, her withered lips would murmur the words, "Glory be to the Father," and she would feel as a wayworn traveller feels in a hot and desert country when he comes across a little fountain of fresh water springing up in his path. His journey is not over, but the living waters give him strength to go on with it.

So bad a name did Humphrey and his eldest son bear in the parish, as being idle and drunken vagabonds, that it overshadowed Ruth and Ishmael, and they found themselves banished by it from all intercourse with decent and friendly neighbors. Ishmael did not feel it until he went to the village school, where the other children were warned against Humphrey Medway's boy. The women who worked with Ruth in the fields kept aloof

---

1 Mark 10:45.
2 Genesis 16:11.
3 Cheep—to give expression to in a chirping tone.

from her; not so much because they were better off than she was, but because she was so silent in her ways. Thus there was no companionship for them but in each other; and it was sufficient. It was enough for Ruth to think of her boy all day, and to hear his regular healthful breathing beside her all night; and for Ishmael, the woods that lay all around his home gave him never-ending occupation and delight.

But though they were without friends, they were not without an enemy. The nearness of the low hovel to the woods was enough to arouse the suspicions of the squire's gamekeeper, even if he had had no reason to dislike Humphrey Medway and his family. But, before Ishmael was born, there had existed a bitter hatred between Nutkin, the gamekeeper, and young Humphrey, Ishmael's eldest brother. Humphrey had succeeded in winning away from Nutkin the girl he had wished to make his wife; and, though the keeper had himself married shortly afterwards, he had never forgiven the offence, or ceased to hold him and all belonging to him in bitter enmity. The very name of Medway was hateful to his ears. Of late, too, Ishmael had won two or three prizes at the village school over the head of his own boy, who was about the same age, and who lamented loudly over his defeat by old Humphrey's despised son.

Yet in spite of all Nutkin's efforts he had been unable to dislodge old Humphrey from the miserable hut. The rent of a shilling a week was paid punctually by Ruth, who would rather have gone without food than omit its regular settlement, since nothing else could keep her drunken husband and herself from the parish workhouse. The farmer who held a lease of the lime-kiln and the hut found her work on his farmstead and showed her some little favor. So all the keeper could do was to suspect and to watch, ready to take advantage of any trespass that could be punished by the law.

For thirteen years now Ruth had worked upon the Willows Farm; and many a hot summer day had Ishmael, when a baby, lain all day long under the hedgerows, carefully swathed in an old shawl, while his mother toiled in the harvest fields. He had himself begun to earn a few pence as soon as he could scare crows from the springing corn, or could help to tend the sheep in the chilly days of spring during the lambing season. For the last two years his father had been grumbling at his being an idle mouth to feed, though it was rarely Ruth saw a penny of his money, and it had been with difficulty that she had been able to keep her boy at school. But now the time was come when Ishmael must cease to be a child, and must begin to get his own living by regular work. Mr. Chipchase, the farmer, had consented to try him as waggoner's boy, and had promised, if he was a good and steady lad, to "make a man of him."

"Mother," said Ishmael, as they sat together on their door-sill in the long, light June evening, listening to the cuckoo and the thrushes singing in the woods, "I told teacher I'm going to service on Monday; and she says I may take little Elsie into the woods tomorrow, and she'll give us dinner to eat there, for me as well as her, mother; because she says I've always been a good boy at school, and she's sorry to lose me."

"I'm glad she's sorry to lose thee," said Ruth; "and if thee weren't to sleep at home every night, I hardly know what I could do without thee, Ishmael. I almost wish thee were a tiny little lad once again."

"When I'm a man," he answered eagerly, "you shan't ever go out working in the fields, or tire yourself, mother. We'll never, never leave here, because there's no place like it; but I'll get the master to let me build a better house, that'll keep you warm and dry, and we'll live together till we die: won't we, mother?"

"Please God!" she said softly, with a smile on her brown face, as she thought how much earlier she must die than the young lad, little more than a child, who sat beside her.

"I should think it would please God," answered Ishmael, in a quiet voice. "He doesn't want us to be always very poor, poorer than other folks, mother?"

"Nay, I don't know," she replied; "His own Son was born in a stable, and died upon the cross, with folks mocking at Him. I don't know what thee and me have to go through, Ishmael. We can only say, 'Please God!'"

It was late before Ishmael mounted the ladder to the close loft overhead and crept into his bed on the floor under the low thatch. But it was after midnight when Ruth, with her wrinkled yet sinewy arms, helped her drunken husband from one rung to another, fearful every night lest her strength should fail her, and that he might fall, crippled or lifeless, on the floor below.

"Thank God!" she always cried in the depth of her soul, when his sluggish and leaden feet were safely planted on the floor above.

Chapter 2

IN THE WOODS

The village schoolmistress, Mrs. Clift, knew Ruth well, for she had employed her as her laundress from the time she had taken charge of the school; and no linen could be sweeter and whiter than that which Ruth washed, and dried in the sun on the gorse bushes growing about the old limekiln. Ishmael had been one of the most constant and least troublesome of her scholars; and she was willing to mark her approbation of him by intrusting her little girl to his care for a long day in the Limekiln Woods.

The spring had come slowly on during May, and though it was already June, the trees were not yet in full leaf. The delicate network of boughs overhead still kept many an open space for the sunshine to stream through, and the half-transparent leaves glistened with a green light. There was no thick tangle of burdock and thistle at present to catch their feet and hinder them as they strolled along under the hazel bushes. Here and there patches of bluebells covered the dusky earth; and in a few rare spots, known to Ishmael, white lilies of the valley were growing amid their broad green leaves. No very tall or massive forest trees grew in the thin soil; but now and then an elm or an oak, somewhat stunted, spread out its crooked branches; and there were clumps of larches, tall and thin, growing in close companionship, with their pointed tops piercing the sky. And what a sky it was! A deeper blue than the bluebells under the hazels, with little clouds scattered over it whiter than the lilies, some of gleaming brightness, and others of a pearly grey, floating lazily along before the soft, fresh, westerly wind. Ishmael felt a pride in it all, as if the woods, and the flowers, and the sky belonged to himself.

"Sit down and listen, Elsie," he said, throwing himself under an elm tree, and holding his breath for very pleasure, as he strained his ear to catch the different notes of the birds, singing in these early hours of the sunny day. There was the merry whistle of the starling—did Elsie hear that?—and the deep, soft cooing of the wood-pigeons from their great clumsy nests in the fir trees; and the harsh cry of the jay, as he flitted across the open space between some trees, displaying his bright blue wing-feathers. Oftener than any other note, except the chirp of the sparrows, came the deep, grave caw of the rooks, as they sailed by high in the air. Or was not the clear merry song of the thrushes and blackbirds in the bushes all about them the most frequent sound of them all? But Ishmael knew also the note of the kingfisher and the woodpecker, and the plaintive cry of the lapwing, and the call of the little moorhen in the swampy ground, overgrown with water weeds and tall bulrushes. Every sound, loud and low, of the busy woodlands was known to him; but they had never been so sweet to him as now, when, for the first time, he had a companion gazing admiringly into his face as he displayed his knowledge. Elsie was far before him in school; but here she sat with wide-open, wondering eyes, drinking in every word he spoke.

"Oh, Ishmael!" she exclaimed, with a sigh of happiness and

admiration, "I should think nobody in the world knows as much as you!"

Never before had Ishmael had such words spoken to him, and he felt almost dizzy. He began to think what other wonders he could show or tell to her. Yes, there were more wonderful things to disclose to her admiring eyes. The woods were beautiful; but he knew what was hidden underground as well as what lay open to the eye of day. For underneath their feet the earth was honeycombed with long, deserted galleries, and roadways, and tunnels, where ages ago the limestone had been dug, and brought to the surface by level shafts opening on the hill slopes. Far away from the light of the sun, these subterranean paths ran in many windings and twistings. Even on the surface there were indications of them in basin-like hollows of varying depths and sizes, where the treacherous ground had sunk in. Some of these hollows were filled with water, forming little pools, which glistened up to the sun, while others were dry basins green with turf and colt's-foot, amongst which wild strawberries grew. Ishmael and Elsie had busily gathered the small red fruit, and strung it upon long bents of grass, to keep it as a dessert to the dinner they were going to eat in the woods. Ishmael hastily formed a surprise for Elsie. When the right minute came, when she was tired and hungry, and the sun beat hotly upon them, he would take her to the cool shelter of a cave near at hand, where he could show to her the entrance into the old limestone quarry.

They came at length to a broad open glade, stretching far away between two rows of trees, which was the famous spot for shooting-bouts in the autumn, when the squire's visitors spent whole days in sport. Here in the long, untrodden grass lay the old cartridge-cases thrown hastily away last year. Ishmael told Elsie how the cracking of the guns rang all day long, and how the smell of the gunpowder and its thick smoke tainted the sweet air; and how, at night, when all was over, there seemed a sorrowful silence in the wood, as if its timorous inhabitants had been scared into utter terror.

"And the rabbits keep in their burrows," said Ishmael, "and don't come out to play after sunset, like they do other nights— ay, by hundreds and thousands, running after one another, and tumbling about like us on the green when we've a holiday, and you can see their little white pads tossing about in the dusk. If you sit very still they'll come a'most to your feet. And the bats fly about, and the cockchafers, and big white owls, that make no noise when they fly. I'll show you our big owl at home before you go home tonight."

They were sauntering along the glade slowly, when suddenly, from under their very feet, as it seemed to Elsie, there sprang up, with a loud whirr and a great fluttering of wings, a pheasant which had been sitting close on her nest among the long grass till their feet nearly touched her. Elsie uttered a little scream of fright; but Ishmael went down on his knees in a moment, parting the tangled grass which hid the nest. There lay a cluster of brown eggs, ten of them, packed closely together, and warm with the brooding heat of the mother-hen.

"Oh!" cried Elsie eagerly, "can't we have some of them for dinner? Only we can't cook them, you know, without a fire and a saucepan."

"Ay, but we can!" answered Ishmael, proud of doing what seemed impossible to his companion; "we can make a fire, and roast 'em in the ashes. We won't take more than four, two apiece; and I can tell which are the newest laid. See, I've got a match in my pocket, and we'll pick some sticks, and light a fire in a place I know of, where nobody can ever find us."

Gathering up the sticks as they went along, he led Elsie to his cave. It was situated about half-way down a steep slope which was overgrown with hazel bushes and brambles. The low archway of the entrance was little more than a yard high, and was quite concealed by the brushwood. Within, the roof rose to a good height, and the floor of limestone was dry, forming altogether a pleasant retreat, large enough to hold from twenty to thirty persons. A green twilight reached them through the closely interwoven network of underwood; and a delicious coolness made it the pleasantest place possible, now the sun was so high in the blue sky.

"Look, Elsie," said Ishmael, leading her to the back of the cave, where a small hole, not unlike a large rabbit-burrow, led darkly into some space beyond, "I've crawled through there many a time; and if it wasn't for your frock we'd go now—you and me. Oh, it goes for miles and miles under the wood; and sometimes there's a little bit o' light coming through cracks in the ground; and there are pools all black and still, with just a tiny sparkle on them to show where they are; and there are glistening stones hanging down from the roof, and drops o' water always falling, falling from them. Oh, I wish you were a boy, and could creep in along with me!"

"Oh, couldn't I?" cried Elsie.

"No, it 'ud never do," he said decisively. "Nevermind; I'll light the fire now, and we'll have our dinner."

The fire was quickly kindled, and after it had died down a little, the four eggs were covered over with hot embers, and left to roast. Ishmael had brought a can of sparkling water from a little spring trickling down the rock, whilst Elsie had laid out their dinner. Now she was sitting beside it on a big stone, with her hands lying idly on her lap in simple enjoyment, and her blue eyes gazing out happily on the waving branches outside, whose shadows flickered up to her feet in a constant dance.

"Oh, Ishmael," she cried, "I must say the song mother taught me about 'That's the way for Billy and me.' It seems as if it was made for us; and I'll say them while the eggs are roasting.

"Where the pools are bright and deep,
    Where the grey trout lies asleep,
    Up the river and over the lea,
    That's the way for Billy and me.

Where the blackbird sings the latest,
    Where the hawthorn blooms the sweetest,
    Where the nestlings chirp and flee,
    That's the way for Billy and me.

Where the mowers mow the cleanest,
    Where the hay lies thickest and greenest,
    There to trace the homeward bee,
    That's the way for Billy and me.

Where the hazel-bank is steepest,
    Where the shadow falls the deepest,
    Where the clustering nuts fall free,
    That's the way for Billy and me.

Why the boys should drive away
    Little maidens in their play,
    Or love to banter and fight so well,
    That's a thing I never could tell.

But this I know, I love to play
    Through the meadow, among the hay,
    Up the water, and over the lea,
    That's the way for Billy and me."[1]

---

1 This lovely little song is by James Hogg, the Ettrick Shepherd, and is not as well known as it deserves to be.

But Elsie had scarcely finished the last line when she saw the branches before her slowly parted, and a man's head bent down and looking into their cave. It was a brown, sunburnt, rugged face: she knew it well enough, but she had never liked it, and at this moment it filled her with vague terror. Ishmael was kneeling by the red and smouldering fire, and touching the eggs with the tips of his fingers. So absorbed was he that he did not notice the darkening of the green twilight as the gamekeeper came stooping under the archway; and he laughed a low, quiet laugh of delight as he took one of the eggs from its hot bed.

"That one's done, Elsie!" he exclaimed gaily.

"What's done?" asked Nutkin's harsh voice close beside him. "I saw the smoke from your fire, you young rascal, and I came to see what mischief you're up to. What, pheasant's eggs! pheasant's eggs! Would nothing else serve you for your dinner?"

Ishmael knelt, unable to stir, and gazing up aghast into the gamekeeper's angry yet triumphant face. What could he say? There were the eggs in the ashes between them; he could not even drop the one he was holding in his outstretched hand. He felt as if he could neither move nor speak. He had no right to those eggs; they were stolen; but he had not thought of that when Elsie had uttered her childish wish.

"I suppose you know," said Nutkin very slowly, as if he meant every word to strike home, "that I shall take you to gaol for this?"

"Oh no, no!" cried Elsie, in an agony of fright; "we didn't know it was any harm, did we, Ishmael? The eggs were on the ground, and we might have trodden on them. Don't send us to gaol!"

"It's not you, only this young scoundrel," continued Nutkin; "you may have to go before the justices, but it's him as'll go to gaol for poaching and stealing. I've told the squire scores of times, and now he'll believe me. Get up, you rascal, and come along with me."

Suddenly Ishmael broke into a loud and bitter cry, which rang through the cave, and seemed to be muttered back again from the old quarry.

"Oh, what will mother say when she hears of it?" he cried.

"And what will father say?" jeered the gamekeeper, "and brother Humphrey? We'll take care you don't grow up a drunkard and a disgrace to the parish, like them, my fine fellow. Come along! Elsie, you run home to your mother, and tell her to be more careful who you keep company with another time. The squire'll believe me now."

So saying, he dragged Ishmael out of the cave, and taking a strong rope from his pocket, he knotted it into a sort of handcuff, by which he bound the lad fast to him. Elsie followed them, sobbing, to the white dusty road leading to Uptown, where there was a police station; and then, sadly watching them out of sight, she went home almost heartbroken to her mother.

Chapter 3

SATURDAY AND SUNDAY

Ruth had been hard at work all day hoeing thistles. Many a time she lifted up her eyes to the green woods where Ishmael and Elsie were at play, and recalled the rare days of holiday like it which she had had when she was young. The thought of the children's pleasure made her own work lighter; and though she was tired enough when she heard the church clock strike the hour for leaving the field, she walked along briskly under the hedge, to be home the sooner. Elsie and Ishmael would be fine and hungry before she could get tea ready; and Mrs. Chipchase had promised her some buttermilk, to make them some buttermilk pikelets for a treat. There was a pleasant stir and agitation in Ruth's mind, yet there was a vague disquiet mingled with the pleasure. Ishmael was about to cease to be a child, and was stepping into the perils and duties of boyhood, that dangerous crisis in which she had seemed to lose all her other children. He was about to escape from under her wing, and flutter away, like these little half-fledged hedge-sparrows which were twittering and hovering all along the thorn bushes. Her other boys and girls seemed to care no more for their poor home than the nestlings of this year will care for the old nest next spring. But Ishmael was not like the others, who had all taken after their father, and only thought of their mother as a drudge to slave for them. She had not been as good a mother to them, she said to herself; but then she had not believed in God as she did now. How marvelously good He had been to her to give her such a son as Ishmael, when she was a weary, worn-down, grey-haired woman!

Mrs. Chipchase nearly filled Ruth's large brown pitcher with buttermilk, and gave her two or three spoonfuls of tea in a screw of paper. Ruth was a favorite with her, as being a quiet, harmless old woman, and she lingered a moment at the door to speak a word or two to her.

"Mind Ishmael's here in time of a morning," she said, "for the master's very particular."

"I'm sure," answered Ruth falteringly, "as I don't know how to thank you and the master for taking him. It'll be the makin' of him, I know; and he's a good lad, ma'am, God bless him!"

It was seldom Ruth uttered so many words together, except to Ishmael; but her heart was full. The farmhouse was a homely place, but there was a rude abundance about it which she seemed to feel for the first time, as if she also had a share in it. She stood at the kitchen door, and could see the big table at which Ishmael would eat, where a ploughboy was now sitting, deeply absorbed in the contents of a huge basin, which had been filled up from a big iron pot hanging a little way above the fire. The smell of the good broth reached her, and seemed to promise that Ishmael would grow a strong, hale man, when he could always satisfy his hunger. "He hath satisfied the hungry with good things,"[1] she murmured to herself, as she took up her brown pitcher, and with a curtsey to the mistress turned to go away.

"Ruth Medway!" shouted a loud, rough voice from the far

1 See Luke 1:53.

end of the farmyard, "Nutkin the keeper's been and hauled Ishmael to gaol for stealing pheasant's eggs in the wood!"

"There's the master come home!" cried Mrs. Chipchase. "Whatever is he shouting, Ruth?"

Ruth was still standing with a smile on her wrinkled face, but it died away as the meaning of the words reached her brain. The sky grew black, and the sunshine fled away; a dizziness seized her, which made the solid ground she stood on reel beneath her. The loud crashing of her brown pitcher, as it slipped from her hand and broke into a hundred fragments on the stone causeway, brought her back to her senses.

"What's the matter?" asked Mrs. Chipchase, running to the door, which her husband had now reached.

"Matter enough!" he answered. "Here's our new waggoner's lad, that was to come on Monday morning, taken off to gaol for poaching. Nutkin caught Ishmael and Elsie roasting eggs in the wood—pheasant's eggs, stolen from the nest! There's no chance of him getting off, for the squire's mad after game; and Nutkin swears he'll lock him up out of harm's way. I'm sorry for you, Ruth, to have such a husband and family. I did think Ishmael was going to be a comfort to you in your old age. But the lad knew better, and he's no excuse."

"It was naught but a lad's trick," said Mrs. Chipchase, "such as anyone 'ud do. Ishmael never stole an egg of mine, when I set him to gather them. Our own boys never brought in more than he did. He's as honest as the day, I'm sure."

"Thank you kindly, ma'am," murmured Ruth, turning away and walking slowly down the causeway towards home, with a bowed head and feeble feet. How heavily her sixty years seemed to weigh upon her all at once! How rough the road was, which she had trodden so many hundreds of times in all kinds of weather, to earn her own bread and Ishmael's! Was she half-blind, that everything looked so dim? And where had all the merry sounds of the summer evening gone to? There was a sort of numbness and stupor over her mind, until she found herself trying to fit the old key into the lock of her poor hut, the home Ishmael had never yet left for a single night. He was not coming home tonight!

She sunk down on the door-sill, and swayed herself to and fro in mute despair. No tears came to her eyes, for she was old, and her tears were exhausted; but she sobbed heavily again and again, and yet again. There was no hope in her heart. She thought of Nutkin's enmity and her husband's bad character. The rector's family had gone away to foreign parts for six months, and a stranger, who knew nothing of Ishmael, was taking the duty of the parish. The squire could not be reached, for Nutkin's influence was all-powerful with him. No, there was no chance for Ishmael.

To be in prison! Home was poor enough; she felt all at once what a dark, miserable, empty hovel it was. But if Ishmael could only be within, it would be a true home to both of them. She sat down on the desolate hearth, and tried to think of God; but she could think of no one but Ishmael yet. Her soul was in the deepest depths. All night long she lay awake. The little bed on the floor beside her was empty for the first time, and her ear listened in vain for Ishmael's quiet breathing. Her husband had come home so drunk that she had not dared to get him up the ladder, and he was lying in a dead sleep on the floor below. Over and over again she counted her nine children on her fingers, some dead and some living, and a heavy sob broke from her lips as she whispered "Ishmael." She had mourned over her dead, and grieved over her living children who had forsaken her; but no sorrow had been like this sorrow. None of them had ever been in prison, and now it was her youngest and dearest—yes, and her best—who was fallen into deep disgrace. When the morning came, her heart turned sick at the thought of going to church, and Humphrey with an oath forbade her to go to Uptown after Ishmael. Ishmael would not be in the singing gallery; and how could she sing "Glory be to the Father" while he was in prison?

All the morning Humphrey, sitting by the wood-fire, to make sure that Ruth obeyed him, was cursing Ishmael as a disgrace; but she did not answer a word. She had kept silence so long that she hardly knew how to talk, except to Ishmael. It was a relief to her when her husband took himself off in the afternoon, and left her in solitude as well as silence. She was sitting alone, with her wrinkled face hidden in her hands—deaf, blind, and mute to everything but her trouble, when she felt the warm pressure of loving arms round her neck. For a moment she thought it was Ishmael, but looking up she saw the face of Elsie. Her mother was standing near, and when Ruth rose to drop a curtsey to the schoolmistress, she took her hard cramped hand between both of her own, and, bending forwards, kissed the old woman's brown cheek. Ruth's face flushed a little, and a strange feeling of surprise and pleasure flashed across the darkness of her grief.

"I want you to get a cup of tea for me," said Mrs. Clift.

It was something for Ruth to do; and as she busied herself in kindling her swift-burning fire, and filling her small tin kettle from the well, for a few fleet moments she forgot Ishmael. But she could eat nothing when the tea was ready, though Elsie had brought some dainty tea-cakes in order to tempt her appetite.

"I have been up to the Hall, and seen Mr. Lansdowne," said Mrs. Clift, as they sat together at the rough little table. "Elsie has to go before the magistrates tomorrow at Uptown; and I went to speak for poor Ishmael. But there's not much hope, Ruth. Mr. Lansdowne tells me Nutkin says Ishmael has infested the woods since his very babyhood, and all the village thinks him to be in league with poachers. That's not the truth, I know."

Ruth shook her head in sorrowful denial.

"I told the squire so," said the schoolmistress softly; "and he answered, women never could be made to believe that poaching was a crime. I did say I couldn't call taking a few eggs from a wild bird's nest any great sin—not bad enough for a young lad to be sent to gaol for. He said it was not only that, but all the Medways were a plague and a pest in the parish; and it would be a kindness to check Ishmael at the outset. Ruth, I'm more grieved than I can tell you."

Again Ruth shook her grey head in silence.

"I've been thinking how lonely you are, and how you have to bear the sins of your husband and sons," said Mrs. Clift; "and it seems to me that to think of our Lord's life here is the only thing to comfort you. Do you remember the words, 'He is despised and rejected of men; a Man of sorrows, and acquainted with grief: and we hid as it were our faces from Him; He was despised, and we esteemed Him not'?"[1]

The quiet voice speaking so gently to her ceased for a few minutes; and Ruth covered her troubled face again with her hands. It was the Lord Jesus who had been despised and rejected of men, as she was by her neighbors. He had been "a Man of sorrows, and acquainted with grief," more deeply than she was. Did her old companions in the village hide as it were their faces from her? Nay, all the world had hid their faces from Him who died to save them. Even on the cross those that passed by reviled Him, wagging their heads; and the chief priests and elders, and the thieves crucified with Him, had mocked and jeered at Him.

"'Surely He hath borne our griefs, and carried our sorrows,'"[2]

---

1 Isaiah 53:3.
2 Isaiah 53:4.

resumed the quiet, gentle voice. "'He was wounded for our transgressions: the chastisement of our peace was upon Him; and with His stripes we are healed.'"[1]

She was not bearing her griefs alone, then, as she had fancied during the long dark night. The Lord Himself had carried her sorrows. He had been wounded for her transgressions, and for Ishmael's. A healing sense of His love and compassion and fellow-feeling was stealing over her aching heart.

"'All we like sheep have gone astray,'" went on the soothing voice; "'we have turned every one to his own way; and the Lord hath laid on Him the iniquity of us all. He was oppressed, and He was afflicted, yet He opened not His mouth: He is brought as a lamb to the slaughter, and as a sheep before her shearers is dumb, so He openeth not His mouth.'"[2]

Dumb, and opening not His mouth! Was not that again like herself? She could not cry aloud, and speak many words, and make her grief known to every ear. It was true. Jesus Christ had lived her life of sorrows, and grief, and scorn, and silence. Her head was bowed down still, but her heart was lifted up. The suffering Son of God made it easier for her to bear her own suffering.

It was growing dusk now, and the schoolmistress bade her good-night; but Ruth would go a little way on the road with her. When she returned to her lonely home, she lingered for a minute, trembling and reluctant to re-enter its dark solitude. It had always been her custom, since Ishmael was a baby in her arms, to sing, "Glory to Thee, my God, this night," as the last thing before he went to bed, except when Humphrey happened to be at home, which was very seldom. She had not thought of it last night, the first time that Ishmael had been away from her. But the thought crossed her mind, and could not be driven

---

1 Isaiah 53:5.
2 Isaiah 53:6, 7.

away from it, that, maybe, this Sunday evening he was singing it alone in his cell at Uptown. The tears, which had not come last night, stood in her dim eyes, as, sitting down in her old chair by the dark hearth, she sang the hymn right through, in a low and faltering voice, which could hardly have been heard beyond the threshold.

Chapter 4

THE MAGISTRATES' MEETING

Uptown was not worthy of the name of town; it could hardly be called a large village. But it was the center of a wide agricultural district, and a small market was held in it once a week, chiefly for the sale of butter and eggs, as the farmers carried their corn to a more important market farther away, in the county-town. A magistrates' meeting was held at Uptown at stated intervals, and there was a police station just outside the village, provided with two cells, but seldom occupied, in one of which Ishmael had been safely kept since noon-day on Saturday.

Heavy-hearted still, though with a fund of secret courage bearing her up, Ruth entered Uptown on the Monday morning. There was more stir than usual about the single street, as there always was on the days when the magistrates came to hear the trivial cases which awaited their judgment. Round the inn where the justices' room was, there were several groups of some-what discreditable folks hanging about in readiness. Nutkin was within the inn-yard, eagerly talking to one of the magistrates, who had arrived before the others and had just dismounted from his horse. Ruth saw him, but it was as if she did not see him, so absorbed was her whole soul in watching for Ishmael to come along the road between the town and the police station. She was half unconscious of the increasing crowd and stir, as the magistrates rode in one after another, and the magistrates' clerk bustled down from his house with his blue bag full of papers. Mrs. Clift had arrived, too, with Elsie; and Squire Lansdowne was gone into the large room of the inn; but she only half knew it. At last Ishmael appeared, walking beside a policeman, who kept his hand tightly on his collar, as if to remind him it was of no use to try to escape. But could this sullen, scowling lad, with rough, uncombed hair and tear-stained face, be Ishmael? He was close beside her, yet he never raised his eyes; and he would have passed her by if she had not cried out in a very lamentable voice, "O Ishmael, Ishmael!"

"It's my mother," he said, as the policeman tightened his grasp of his collar. "Don't you come inside, mother dear. It 'ud do no good, and it 'ud make me cry. You go home again, now you've seen me to say good-bye. You'll loose me to kiss my mother?" he added, looking at the policeman.

"Ay, if you're sharp about it," he answered.

For a minute the young boy, scarcely more than a child, and the bent, grey-haired woman stood with their arms fondly cling-ing about each other. Ruth felt as if she could not let him go; it seemed but a few days since he was but a baby in her bosom; and now he was a prisoner charged with an offence against the laws of his country. But Ishmael loosened his hands and let himself be led away inside the magistrates' room. Then she sat down on the lowest step of a horse-block below its open window, through which she could hear the hum of voices coming indistinctly to her ear. How long it was she did not know, but a gaily dressed, flaunting young woman came to her at length, and spoke in a pitying tone.

"Don't you take on, Mrs. Medway," she said. "You're a good woman, I know, but luck's agen you. Nutkin was very hard on him; and they've give him three months in the county gaol."

"Is it my Ishmael?" she asked, looking up with a wandering and vacant expression in her eyes.

"To be sure," answered the young woman. "'Ishmael Medway, thirteen years of age; three months for stealing pheasant's eggs.'"

Ruth heard no more, saw nothing more. But bending forward, as if to lift herself upon her feet, she fell heavily on the pavement in a deep swoon. There was a crowd clustering about her when Ishmael was marched out of the inn by the policeman; he looked round in vain for a last glance at his mother's face.

"It were best for her to go away," he said to himself, with a sob; "but I should ha' liked to ha' seen her again."

He felt as if he were going to die in the prison to which they were sending him, and as if he should never see his mother's face again. His young soul was in a bewilderment of grief and amazement. He had heard himself described as an incorrigible thief and poacher. Everything had gone against him: the notorious character of his father and elder brothers; his own admission of having haunted the woods until he knew every spot in them; even his tearful confession that he knew he had no right to the eggs, and did not know why he should take them then for the first time. All had been against him. He was going away to gaol, a shame and disgrace to his poor mother. Today, too; the very day he was to have begun to earn his own living, and relieve her from the burden he had been upon her. He would be a worse trouble to her than any of the others had been, even than his father, who came home every night either drunk or angry. What could he ever do to make it up to her now? He could do nothing better than to die.

It was late before Ruth reached home in the evening, and she found her husband awaiting her return, sober and sullen; a hard, tyrannical old man, who looked upon her as a silent and spiritless drudge.

"So," he exclaimed, as she stepped feebly and weariedly over the threshold, "this is what it's come to: thy fine lad's got hisself into gaol! This comes o' book-learnin' and psalm-singin', eh? He brings shame on all on us. Ne'er a one on us was iver up afore the justices till now; and they say at the 'Labour in Vain' as he's got three months. And serve him right, I say! I takes sides with Nutkin, and th' squire, and the justices, as are ivery one on 'em gentlemen. If I'd a bit o' land, I'd hang every poacher as set foot on it. And a young little lad o' his age! What'll he be when he's a man? I'd ha' sent him to Botany Bay, I would. I'm on the side o' justice. And if ever Ishmael crosses o'er that door-sill agen, I'll thresh him to within an inch o' his life! I'll break ivery bone in his body! And thine, too," he shouted, with growing fury, "if thee don't open that cursed mouth o' thine, and say somethink!"

"I'm ill, Humphrey," she answered meekly; "I swoonded away dead when they told me on it."

"Swoonded!" he repeated sneeringly; "don't tell me. It's only born ladies as can do that, not a workin' woman like thee. But swound or no swound, just hearken to my words. Ishmael niver sets his foot over yon door-sill. I'll harbor no poachers or gaol-birds under my roof."

Very quietly Ruth went on lighting the fire and boiling the kettle. It was a relief to her to be at home again, out of the stir and buzz of the little town, and out of sight of inquisitive eyes. Even her husband's threats and jeers could not altogether spoil the sense of having found rest at her own fireside. And when he was gone, the unbroken silence of the dark hut suited her. Her harassed soul could recollect itself now. Even in dense darkness our eyes by eager gazing begin to see a little, and so in the deepest trouble the soul by its earnest yearning towards God begins to discern light. As Ruth sat alone in the dark hut, there came back to her memory the old story in the Bible from which she had taken a name for her youngest boy. She thought of Hagar in the wilderness, a runaway slave, fleeing from her mistress, and how God heard her affliction; and how once more she was driven into the wilderness, wandering up and down homeless, until her son Ishmael was dying of thirst, and his mother cast him under a shrub to die, and went away out of sight—a good way off—lest she should see the death of her child; and how God heard the voice of the lad, and once again sent His angel to succor Hagar. Ruth shut her aching and swollen eyelids with a feeling of comfort and awe, as she whispered, "'Thou God seest me.'"[1]

Yes, God saw; God knew. There was unspeakable consolation in that. She felt no bitterness of heart, even against Nutkin. She had nothing to say against the law that had sent Ishmael to prison. She did not try to justify her boy; he had done wrong, though in light-heartedness and thoughtlessness, not in malice. None of these things occupied her simple mind. God had seen all; and He knew all about it. It was in that thought she was to find consolation and strength. She must endure, as seeing Him who is invisible.

---

1 Genesis 16:13.

Chapter 5

TURNED ADRIFT

The hay-harvest and the corn-harvest, with their long hours of labor in the sunshine, passed by; and Ruth was one of the busiest of the women working on Chipchase's farm. No one saw much change in her, for she had always been a silent, inoffensive woman, minding her own business, and leaving other folks alone. But when harvest was ended, and the shooting season begun, the term of Ishmael's imprisonment was nearly over. Nutkin and his assistant-keepers were very busy about the woods, watching them all night, whilst all day long the crash of guns could be heard far and near. It was not a good time for Ishmael to be coming home; there was too much to put her husband in mind of his threats, and to keep his anger hot against his son. But surely he could not be so hard as to turn Ishmael out of doors when the law let him go free!

"Ishmael's time's up tomorrow," she said in a tremulous voice one evening, with a deep anxiety she was striving to conceal.

"Ay," answered Humphrey slowly, "that's what Nutkin says. So I up to the Hall this mornin' early, and I says to th' squire, 'Squire, I've been an honest man all my life; and I've worked on your hedges many a year; and I'm not a-goin' to harbor no poacher in my home. There's that lad o' mine, that's been a disgrace to me, a-comin' out o' the county gaol tomorrow. He'll niver set his foot o'er my door-sill, I promise you.' The squire says, 'As you choose, Humphrey. Go into the kitchen, and get a draught o' ale.' And good ale it was; a sight better nor that at the 'Labour in Vain.' I'm not the man to drink the squire's good ale, and go agen him in any way."

"Thou'lt never turn the lad adrift on the world?" cried Ruth.

"Adrift! He's big enough to shift for himself," said Humphrey doggedly. "The squire could get us turned out o' here neck-and-crop if he chosen; and what 'ud become of me, if we had to go to the workhouse? The squire won't have no poacher harbored close to his woods; and who's to save me from goin' into the house in my old age, eh? Me, as can't live without my drop o' good ale, often and regular. I tasted the beer in the workhouse once. No; Ishmael niver sets his foot o'er that door-sill agen! And now thou knows it, and can make the best on it."

Ruth had a sleepless night again, as if the first bitterness of her sorrow had come back upon her with tenfold power. Early as the dawn came the next morning, she was up before it, making a bundle of all Ishmael's coarse clothing, the scanty outfit she had scraped together for him three months ago, when he was going out to earn his own living. Mrs. Chipchase was taking her butter to market in the county town, and had offered to carry Ruth with her in the gig, that she might meet Ishmael at the gate of the county gaol. She saw little enough of the dusty highroad along which they drove, or of the bustling streets thronged with a concourse of market people. It was only when she came within sight of the gaol that she seemed to wake up from a brown study and get her wits about her again. It stood outside the town, amid green fields—a large, square, ugly building, surrounded by strong and black stone walls. Small round windows, closely barred and grated, looked out like hoodwinked eyes over the lonely fields. Ruth felt herself shivering, though the September sun was shining in an unclouded sky, as she looked up, and wondered which one of those gloomy windows had lighted Ishmael's cell. But before she could reach the heavy gate she saw sauntering down the path from the gaol, creeping with sluggish footsteps and a bowed-down head, her boy, Ishmael himself.

"Mother," he cried, "mother!"

He threw himself into her arms, laughing and crying at the same moment. Ruth could not weep; but she held him fast in her arms, until he lifted up his head to look into her dear face. There was no one near to see them; they were as much alone as in their own quiet woods; only that grim and ugly building looked down upon their meeting with its hollow eyes. She drew him away to a lonely spot under its walls; and they sat down together on the grass, whilst, with her trembling hands, she untied the little packet of home-made bread, baked in their own oven, which she had brought for them to eat together, before they had to part again.

"I never meant any harm, mother," he said, when their meal was over. "I never thought of anything save little Elsie wishing for 'em. But I know it was poaching; and oh, mother, it 'ill turn up against me all my life."

"I'm afeared so, lad," she answered, sighing. "But hast thee asked God's forgiveness, Ishmael?"

"Often and often," he replied eagerly. "Mother, I never forgot to sing, 'Glory to Thee, my God, this night'; only I sang it low, in a whisper, like I used to do when father was at home. I thought you'd be singing it as well, mother."

"Ay," she said softly; "thank God I could sing it after the first evenin', Ishmael."

"When I get home," he went on, "I'll go up to the Hall and ask the squire to forgive me; I'll beg and pray of him; and if he will, maybe I can go to work with Mr. Chipchase, like I was to go before I came here."

"He's got another waggoner's boy," answered his mother; "and thee'rt not to go home with me, but do thy best away from home. Father won't hear of it; and maybe the squire 'ud get us turned out altogether if thee comes home. But if God has forgiven thee ———"

"Not go home with you, mother?" he cried.

"No," she said, half sobbing, "no! But God sees; God knows. Jesus Christ had not where to lay His head, and had to wander about without a home. Ishmael, I want thee to believe that God sees us always; and He loves us, in spite of it seeming as if He didn't take any notice of us. Oh, if I thought God didn't know and didn't care, my heart 'ud break. I'd go down to the river yonder, and just drown myself. But some day He'll find us a home again, thee and me."

She had never spoken so passionately before, even to him; and he was startled, gazing into her agitated face with wondering eyes. Then he looked back at the dreary gaol, his last dwelling-place. There seemed to be no place for him in the whole world now he had been in there.

"Where can we find a home again, mother?" he asked at last; "there's no place like home."

"Up there!" she said, lifting her dim eyes to the great sky above them; "if God gives us no other home here in this world, He's got one ready there for thee and me. 'Let not your heart be troubled: ye believe in God, believe also in Me. In My Father's house are many mansions; I go to prepare a place for you.'[1] That's what Jesus said. He's preparing a place for us, Ishmael;

1 John 14:1, 2.

and we must not trouble our hearts too much. Only we must go on believing in Him."

"I'll try, mother," he said, putting his hand in hers; and they sat there, not speaking much, but with hands closely clasped, till the chiming of the church clocks in the town behind them reminded Ruth there was still something to be done. A place must be found for Ishmael to sleep in that night, and if possible to stay at till he could get work to do.

It was hard work leaving him, so far away from her, to loiter about the streets and pick up any stray job that might fall in the way of a boy with a doubtful character. Her mother's heart told her but too plainly how precarious such a life must be. Only a few months ago he was still a child; even yet, in happier homes, he would be reckoned among the children, to be punished, indeed, for his faults, but not to be thrust into want and temptation. But Ishmael was to fight in the thickest of the battle, bereft of his good name, and removed from all good companionship. Yet Ruth had hope and faith. She worked harder than ever, never taking a day's rest, that she might save a few pence every week to send to his help. She knew he was almost always hungry; often pinched with cold; ragged and nearly barefoot at all times; scarcely able to pay for a shelter night after night. He roamed about the country from farmstead to farmstead, doing any odd work the farmers would trust him with, and sleeping in any outhouse or broken shed he could find open. But he failed in getting a settled place; there were too many boys of good character who wanted to set their foot on the first step of the ladder.

There was one thing he could not make up his mind to do. He could not put such a distance between himself and his mother as would prevent him seeing her every Sunday. He never failed to steal homewards at the close of the week, lurking about the limekiln or the woods, in hiding from his father, until he could make his presence known to his mother. It was the great solace and enjoyment of her life. She could still wash and mend his clothes for him, and get him a sufficient meal or two, and listen to all that had happened to him during the week. He never crossed the threshold of his old home; but on summer evenings Ruth and he sat together within the tangle of green brushwood behind it, and on winter nights they sheltered themselves under the walls of the old kiln, or, if they needed a roof over their heads, they met in the limestone cave, which most often of all was Ishmael's sleeping-place.

Chapter 6

FIVE YEARS

So five years went on, and still Ishmael was not a man. There was little hope now of his even making a strong, hardy, capable man. The privations he was compelled to undergo had told upon his undersized, thin, and feeble frame. But still more had the anxieties and the mortifications he had to endure borne down his spirit. No one but his mother cared for him. Suspicion dogged him, and the doubtful companions necessity forced upon him strengthened suspicion. He was losing heart, and growing hopeless. His mother had called him Ishmael because the Lord had heard her affliction; but she might have called him Ishmael because every man's hand was against him. Would the day come, dreaded by his mother, when his hand would be against every man?

The last few years had weighed more heavily upon Ruth than ten might have done if Ishmael had been at home. She could no longer help her old husband up the ladder when he came home drunk; and many a night he had lain on the damp floor, groaning with rheumatic pains for want of a strong young arm such as Ishmael's would have been. Still every Sunday brought her a gleam of gladness. As yet Ishmael had not gone astray amid his manifold temptations, and she was comforted for her own sorrow and his. But what would become of him when she was no longer there?

It was a hard trial to her, when she heard Ishmael's call, plaintive and low, sounding round and round the hut through the stillness of a winter's night, and she could not answer it. It would come nearer and nearer, until it seemed as if it were under the very eaves; but if her husband was crouching over the fire she dared not even open the door to look out. In the black darkness outside the little casement she could see for a moment the dim outline of her boy's white face gazing through the lattice panes; and then the long, low, plaintive cry grew fainter, and died away in the woods behind.

"I must tell Nutkin of that owl," said old Humphrey peevishly.

At last Ruth could go out no more to her hard work, but lay still and almost helpless in her close loft, scarcely able to creep down the ladder to the hearth below. Old Humphrey could not understand that she was no longer the willing drudge she had been so long. That she should get free from him by death never once crossed his dull brain, soddened by drink. Many a moan he made over his wife's idleness in the sanded kitchen of the "Labour in Vain," where he sat now on a corner of a bench farthest from the fire, having only a few pence to spend; he who in better days had been welcome to the best seat, and been most lavish with his money.

But whenever Sunday came, new life seemed to visit Ruth. Whence the strength arose she could not tell; but it never failed her when she got up from her bed, and crept downstairs, and out into the spring sunshine to meet Ishmael. Everybody knew now, except Humphrey, that Ishmael haunted the old home where his mother was dying; but they took no notice except by carrying food, as they said, for old Ruth, though they knew well she could not eat it. Some of the women offered to do any washing they could for her, and made no remark when Ishmael's clothing was among it. For when we are going down visibly into the dark valley of the shadow of death, those around us look upon us with other eyes, and press upon us some of the kindliness and tenderness which would have made all the pilgrimage of life only a happy journey. Ruth, so long a solitary and sorrowful woman, wondered at the friendliness which gathered about her in her last days.

"It makes home seem sweeter," she said to Ishmael, "to have plenty o' friends, and plenty o' everything else. But if it had always been so I might never ha' thought as dyin' was like goin' home. I always think as if heaven were home now, Ishmael," she added, a faint smile lighting up her wrinkled face.

She was sitting beside him on the old door-sill for the last time, though that they did not know. For when death is drawing near to any one of us we do not always know that the last time is come for the old familiar duties and habits of everyday life. It had been a long, sunny day in May, but now the twilight was coming on, and every minute made her beloved face more thin and shadowy.

"It feels a'most," she went on falteringly, "like when I was a little girl, and 'ud hear father callin' me in from my play. I'm partly afeared to say it, Ishmael; but it's sometimes as if I could hear the blessed Lord callin', 'Ruth, come to Me, and ye shall find rest.' And last night I answered Him out loud, 'Lord, I can't rest because of my lad Ishmael.' And it seemed to me as if there came a low, quiet voice whispering to Me, 'Leave Ishmael to Me. He is My son.' And I said to myself, 'The Lord has heard my affliction again.'"

Ishmael sat silent, with his eyes fastened on the pale yellow light in the sky behind the tops of the trees, across which a bat was flitting to and fro; but he did not see the sunset light or the flight of the bat.

"Ay!" she said almost joyously, "and today I knew He'd heard; for Mrs. Clift and Miss Elsie came to see me; and Ishmael, my lad, they brought grand news for thee. They're going away across the seas, to that country where folks go for a better chance than they've got here; and they've promised to take thee with them; for Mrs. Clift said, 'It was all along of Elsie that Ishmael got into trouble and disgrace, and folks won't think badly of him there; and I'll be like a mother to him,' said Mrs. Clift. And I knew then that God had heard my affliction again."

"Oh, mother!" cried Ishmael, "I couldn't leave thee, never; not if the Queen of England sent for me to go!"

"But oh, my lad," she answered, "if the Lord doesn't take me home afore the time comes for thee to go, thee must leave me. Ay, and I should die happier, knowin' thee were safe away, and havin' a chance to be a good man, than leavin' thee here to be tempted and drove into sin. Ishmael, promise me thee'll go, whether I'm alive or dead, when the time comes. Oh, my dear, dear lad, promise to obey me!'"

"I cannot, mother, I cannot!" he sobbed. "I'll go gladly if thee are dead; but so long as thee can speak to me, and I can look at thee, I cannot go."

"They're not goin' afore hay-harvest," she said softly; "and, please God, I may be dead by then."

But as she lay awake at night, thinking of Ishmael, who was sleeping soundly in his old shelter, the cave in the limestone rock, she wondered what would become of him if she could not prevail upon him to leave her for ever whilst she was still living. There would be no one who loved her to close her dying eyes, and hold her dying hand, and whisper last words of love into her dying ear, if Ishmael were gone. But oh, how gladly would she rather die in utter loneliness if she knew that he was safe, and would have a new start in life!

The days passed slowly away; and the grass grew in the fields around, and blossomed, and ripened for the scythe; but still life seemed to cling to Ruth, weary as she was to die and set Ishmael free. She could no longer come down the ladder which led to the loft, where she lay in darkness; but whenever Humphrey was away, Ishmael was beside her in the darkness, within reach of her hand, as in the old time when he was a child. There was no stint of food for him now, for Mrs. Clift came every day with Elsie, and Mrs. Chipchase sent from the farm, or called in to see Ruth herself, and neither of them came empty-handed. It was only when the time came each day for him to escape out of the way of his father that he felt himself still an exile from his home.

"I'll not leave thee tonight," he said one evening when she seemed worse than he had ever seen her before; "I can't leave thee tonight. Maybe thou'rt dyin'."

"Nay," she answered with a long, low, sad sigh, "nay, Ishmael, there mustn't be a fight 'twixt thy father and thee over my dyin' bed."

"He'll come home drunk," he said almost fiercely, "and I can't leave thee alone with him."

"I'm not afeared to be left alone with thy father," she replied. "He was a good husband to me once, and he'll not be hard with me when I'm dyin'. I wasn't always as good a wife as I might ha' been, and I've a many things to say to him. Hark! they're running to tell thee he's comin' up the lane. Go, Ishmael; kiss me, and go quickly."

"I cannot go!" he cried, clinging to her; "p'r'aps I shall never see thy face again, never! Oh, mother, I cannot go!"

But as he still held her in his arms, and she pushed him

feebly away, Elsie's clear young voice was heard in the kitchen below, calling hurriedly.

"Ishmael," she cried, "little Willie Nutkin is lost in the old quarry behind the cave, and we want you: Nutkin, and the squire and everybody—we all want you."

Chapter 7

HER LAST COMMAND

Ishmael loosed his hold of his mother, but he did not rise from the place where he was kneeling beside her. A faint gleam coming up from the room below lit up Ruth's face as she looked earnestly and searchingly into his.

"I can't quit my mother," he answered, speaking in a loud but forced tone; "she's dyin', and if I go maybe I shall never see her again."

"Ishmael," said Ruth, "thee has never forgiven Nutkin yet."

"No," he muttered, "no; it's been too much to forgive. He drove me away from home; and I'd have been a man by now, instead of a wastrel, if he hadn't been hard on me. Thee'd not ha' worked thyself to death, mother, if it hadn't been for him. No; I've not forgiven him. Let him find his little lad for himself!"

"You must come, Ishmael," called Elsie. "Willie's been missing five hours or more, and we can hear him crying in the old quarry; and nobody knows it like you do; and the opening's too small for a man to crawl through, and it's no use sending in a boy, if any of them would go alone. Oh, come quickly! Suppose he strayed into one of those pools you told me of, and was drowned! Come down this minute!"

But Ishmael did not move, holding his mother's hand between his own, and gazing mournfully into her beseeching face.

"If I bid thee go," she murmured, "thee would not disobey me now I'm dyin'?"

"Don't send me," he cried; "don't bid me go!"

"Nay," she said tenderly, "I'm bound to bid thee, and thee art bound to go. It 'ud be no comfort to see thee nigh me, if I couldn't die happy for thinkin' o' the little lad in the pit. And it's partly because thee hasn't forgiven Nutkin. And if we forgive not men their sins, neither will our Heavenly Father forgive ours. That's what the blessed Lord says. And oh, if thee forgives him, the Lord will forgive thee. Go, Ishmael; I shall see thee again—not here, maybe, but in some better place."

"I'll go," he said, looking into her face very sorrowfully; "but oh, if I never see thee again in this world, it'll seem hard to wait till we get to heaven."

Still Elsie's impatient and entreating voice reached their ears, urging him to make haste, and his mother's sunken eyes were fastened upon him with a look in them as if she was beseeching him to go. It might be the last time he would ever see her face. With a deep and heavy sigh Ishmael stooped to kiss her, and, as if afraid to trust himself to linger another moment, he sprang down the ladder, and, pushing on through bramble and brushwood, quickly reached the entrance of the cave.

It was no longer dark and solitary. Many of the villagers were there, and the glimmer of several lanterns produced a lurid and fitful light. Nutkin knelt at the far end of the cave before the low and narrow inlet, through which, when there was a moment's silence, he fancied he could hear in the black darkness the voice of his child crying.

"The men will be here with pickaxes soon, Nutkin," said the

squire, who stood beside him, "and we'll get the little fellow out in a very short time, my man."

"I'm more afeared of the picks bringing the old roof in than aught else, sir," answered Nutkin, in a voice of despair; "there's been a deal o' heavy rain o' late, and there's been two or three hollows given in above ground, and if the roof gave way betwixt us and the little lad he'd die o' fright before we could dig him out. If the hole was but big enough for a man to creep through! But nobody could creep through a hole no bigger than a rabbit-bury; only a teeny creature like little Willie."

A profound silence followed Nutkin's speech, for no man or woman there could risk the life of any of their boys by sending them into the workings of the old quarry. And amid the silence there was heard plainly enough a low, stifled voice speaking.

"I can crawl through," it said; "I know every step o' the old pit."

"Ishmael Medway!" shouted half a dozen voices joyously; "he's the lad, if there is one."

He felt himself pushed forward to the far end of the cave, where the light was strongest. The thin, stunted, undersized lad, in his tattered clothing, and with his mournful face, stood in front of the squire and of his old enemy, who gazed at him half in shame and half in hope.

"Mother's sent me," he said, touching his old ragged cap to the squire. "She's dyin', and I don't s'pose as I shall ever see her again; but she couldn't die happy with the little lad lost in the pit. And mother says if I forgive him here God'll forgive me, and take me, some day, somewhere, to the place where she's goin'! I slept here last night, and I heard the ground give way. Don't set any picks at work."

Ishmael did not wait for an answer, but lying down on the ground, crept through the narrow, winding tunnel he had often crawled through as a boy. He called back to them when he had reached the shaft, where he could stand upright, and they saw that he had struck a light; but presently all sound and sign of him was lost, and Nutkin and the squire rose from their knees where they had been watching and listening, and the fitful light of the lanterns shone upon the tears in their eyes.

"I'll make a man of that lad," said the squire, in a broken voice.

"God Almighty bring him and Willie safe back," cried Nutkin, sinking down on his knees again, "and I'll treat him as my own son, I will, as long as ever I live! So help me, God!"

So silent for some time was the crowd of villagers now thronging the cave that they could hear the heavy splashes of water falling from the rain-sodden earth into the little pools collected below in the subterranean alleys of the old pit; and once a low rumbling like distant thunder, telling of the earth giving way in one of the many galleries, made them hold their breath in speechless dread, and look anxiously into one another's faces. But, as if Ishmael too had heard it, and wished to reassure them, there came the sound of his voice, calling back to them from the hidden pathways.

"God bless him!" exclaimed the squire, a smile for a moment crossing his anxious and clouded face.

"Ay!" cried Chipchase, "he was as good a lad as ever breathed before he went to gaol for stealing them pheasant's eggs; and old Ruth, his mother, you might trust her in a room full of golden guineas. She's as good an old soul as ever lived. Ishmael said she was a-dying, didn't he, sir?"

"Yes," answered the squire.

"And she'd send him away from her to save Nutkin's little lad!" said Chipchase. "That's what I call being a Christian. Any minute might bring the roof over his head, and bury him alive;

and old Ruth knows it. But if any soul in Broadmoor believes in God, it's Ruth; and, please God, I'll be a better man myself from this day forth."

The farmer's voice trembled as he finished speaking, and he turned his face away from the light, ashamed to let his neighbors see how much he felt.

"Old Ruth's had a hard, bitter life," said Mrs. Chipchase, sobbing; "she was near broken-hearted when Ishmael went to gaol, and she's never been the same woman since. He was like the apple of her eye, Ishmael was; and he'd worse luck than any of her children, thanks to Nutkin, I always said, and always shall say to my dying day. What was a boy's taking a few paltry eggs, I'd like to know?"

"I'll treat him like my own son," muttered Nutkin, not looking up.

"We must make it up to him," added the squire. "If I'd known he was a good lad, he should never have gone to gaol."

"Hush!" cried Elsie, who was standing beside Mrs. Chipchase.

Instantly there was a breathless stillness in the cave, and every eye was turned towards the low outer entrance, through which they could hear the dragging of weary footsteps. Bent almost double, and tottering as if every step must be the last, came old Ruth herself.

"Where's Ishmael?" she asked, looking round at her neighbors' faces with eyes dim and glazed.

Chapter 8

GOING HOME

When Ishmael had obeyed her, and gone away from her deathbed, Ruth had for a little while lain still in utter solitude. After the echo of Ishmael's and Elsie's footsteps had died away, not a sound had reached her ears. She was accustomed to be alone, but this loneliness seemed terrible in her last hours. An unutterable yearning came upon her to see her boy once more, to know what he was doing and what was befalling him. He had gone into danger at her bidding; and until she knew what became of him, she felt as if she could not turn her thoughts even to the God in whom she trusted. If only Humphrey would come home, she would prevail upon him to follow Ishmael to the cave, and bring back word, or send someone to tell her what was going on. How could she die in peace whilst her boy was in instant danger? She lifted herself up, and strained her ear to catch some distant sound of voices or footsteps, but there was nothing save utter silence and solitude.

Then a feverish strength, the strength of the dying, came to her. To be somewhere near where Ishmael was, to have faces about her and hear the voices of her neighbors, seemed absolutely needful to her. With feeble yet hurried hands she dressed herself in the poor old clothing she had laid aside for the last time, and with faltering feet she descended the steep ladder. The fresh air of the evening blowing softly in her face revived her, and made her feel as if it had only been because she had been lying in bed in the hot, dark loft that she had thought herself dying. But as she crept on through the tangle of brushwood, with barely strength enough to part the hazel twigs which beset her path, the numbing hand of death weighed more and more heavily upon her. She heard the voices of her neighbors passing to and fro in the woods, but she could not call loudly enough to make them hear. The thrushes sang in the topmost branches of the trees, where they could yet see the lingering sunset light; but below, her path was all in darkness, and the power of seeing was fading out of her eyes. Half-blind, stumbling over the roots of the trees, fainting with weariness, yet urged on by her passionate love for her son, Ruth reached the cave at last. She was come to die somewhere near where Ishmael was.

"Didn't he say his mother lay a-dying?" exclaimed some of the crowd, as they fell back to make way for her. But as soon as they caught sight of her face by the light of the lanterns they knew that she was dying. She tottered forward with stumbling feet to the end of the cave, and sunk down on the ground, breathing fitfully, whilst her sunken eyes gleamed with a bright light. Nutkin shrunk away in awe of her; but she smiled faintly, and beckoned with her hand that he should watch and listen still at the post he had held since Ishmael had entered the old quarry. But he stood, pale and panic-stricken, looking down upon her as if she had been one come back from the dead.

"Ruth," cried Mrs. Clift, the schoolmistress, coming forward from among the villagers, "how did you get here?"

She sat down on the ground beside her, and drew the grey old head upon her lap; and Ruth looked up thankfully, and summoned all her failing strength to answer.

"I was afeared," she whispered, "never to see Ishmael again. And God helped me. The poor lad 'ud fret so if he never saw me again; and it'll be easier to die here than all alone at home yonder."

"Some of us ought to have thought of you," said the schoolmistress.

"It's best here," she whispered again, "near Ishmael. God's been very good to me all my life; and He's very good to me now I'm dying. I'd rather wait here for him to come back than be anywhere else in the world. Only I shall miss seein' Humphrey, and he was a good husband to me once."

"Ruth Medway," said the squire, speaking slowly and distinctly, that she might hear him, "don't you be troubled about your son. I will see after him, and make a man of him; I promise you solemnly."

Ruth looked up inquiringly into the squire's face—an unfamiliar face, looking blurred and misty to her failing eyes.

"Who is it?" she asked.

"The squire," said the schoolmistress gently.

"I thank you humbly, sir," she said, making a great effort, "but it's too late now, I'm afeared. He's goin' away to a country where there's a better chance for him, as soon as I'm gone. He won't leave me, sir, not as long as I live, if he starves for it. But he'll go as soon as I'm dead."

"I'll make it worth his while to stay at home," said the squire.

"There won't be no home when I'm gone," murmured Ruth; "he's never had a home these five years, like Him that had no place to lay His head."

She closed her eyelids, and lay still, breathing heavily and fitfully, whilst all around her, her old neighbors looked on in mournful silence.

"He's long in coming," she murmured at last, "and it's growing dark, very dark. It's time to sing, 'Glory to Thee;' it'll cheer him, maybe, wherever he is. Only I can't begin."

"She wishes us to sing 'Glory to Thee,'" said Mrs. Clift, looking round at the circle of grave and sorrowful faces surrounding them; "she says it will cheer Ishmael; and it will, if he can only catch a distant sound of it. Some of you belong to the choir; please start it, for I cannot."

Her voice was broken and low, and for the first two or three lines the hymn was sung very tremulously by the villagers. But Ruth's eyes brightened, and a smile broke over her grey and withered face as the familiar strain and the old words reached her dull ear. Her lips moved, and now and then the feeble whispering of a word or two was heard by the schoolmistress. But when the "Praise God, from whom all blessings flow" had been sung in a loud, clear, hearty chorus of every voice, there came, in the silence that followed, a sound as of an echo repeating it in the winding galleries of the old quarry. Ruth lifted up her head, and with sudden strength raised herself to her feet, and leaned against the opening to listen.

"I can hear him," she said joyously, "and I shall see him again! I bid him go, for I was afeared he hadn't forgiven Nutkin; but my heart went with him. He's the only one of 'em all as cares for their old mother; it's the way of young folks," she added, as if to excuse them herself; "but Ishmael was loth to leave me, for fear I should die afore he got back. But I'm here, Ishmael, my lad; I'm close beside thee. Thee and me 'ull see each other again."

She sunk back slowly to the ground; and the neighbors gathered round her again. She was only a poor old toiling woman, for years well known to them all, and little thought of; but there was not one of them who did not grieve for her, or say to themselves how they could have made her hard life a little easier for her. Nutkin knelt down beside her, and his red, sunburnt face looked more full of life and health than ever beside her thin, pinched, pallid features.

"Ruth, forgive me!" he said. "I'd rather have had my right hand shot off, if I'd ha' known it before. It were my wicked hatred as did it. I'd ha' winked at any other lad robbing a pheasant's nest, but I hated the very name o' Medway."

"I never thought myself as there were anything to forgive," she answered. "It's the law, I know; and the justices are wise men. But Ishmael couldn't forgive it, not till now."

But before anyone could speak again there came a shout through the narrow opening, and the sound of a child's voice calling "Father."

Ruth lifted up her head again, and turned her smiling face to the opening.

"He's coming," she said. "God is very good to us."

Yet a few minutes passed away—long, slow minutes—before they could hear Ishmael's footsteps, and his voice speaking gently to the child, who was chattering back again, as if he felt no fear of him, or of the strange place they were in. Very soon the child's tear-stained face was seen crawling back through the archway; yet no one stirred or spoke but Nutkin, who caught his boy in his arms, and hushed him into silence. Ishmael was coming back; and his old mother was leaning forward with her eager dying face, waiting to see him once more. The lad crept out slowly and reluctantly, unwilling to face so many of his old neighbors, and anxious to get away out of sight. His dazzled eyes saw nothing but a cluster of faces about him; and he did not perceive his mother until her feeble voice broke the utter silence which astonished and affrighted him.

"Ishmael!" she called.

"Mother!" he cried in a loud, shrill tone of surprise and

gladness, as he flung himself upon the earth beside her, and put his arm about her, drawing her head down upon his breast.

"I couldn't keep away," she murmured, "and God helped me to come. Be good, Ishmael. God sees us, every one, always. I shall watch for thee on the door-sill—to come into the Father's house boldly—where He's gone to prepare a place—and then we'll be at home again—with Him."

The words dropped slowly, one by one, from the failing lips, which were growing stiff with death, and the bright light in her sunken eyes flickered and died out. But there was still a faint, patient smile on the wrinkled face, and as Ishmael called to her for the last time, in a voice of bitter grief and loneliness, she tried to raise her head and look again into her boy's face. "'Ishmael,'" she whispered, "'because the Lord has heard thy affliction.'"[1]

---

1 Genesis 16:11.

Chapter 9

A NEW HOME

It was a solemn and almost speechless procession that marched through the midnight woods, waking up the sleeping birds in their nests and frightening timid rabbits in their burrows. The moon shone down from the cloudless sky, filling the open spaces with a white light, but deepening the shadows where the hazel bushes grew thickest. Elsie walked beside Ishmael with her hand in his, remembering, oh how keenly, that day five years ago, which had laid the foundation-stone of all his sorrow. But beyond the present sadness there shone a bright hope in the future, though he could not at this moment catch its light. Only a few days, and she and her mother were going to sail for America; and now, when Ishmael had seen his mother's feeble, worn-out body laid in the old churchyard, he would be free to go with them, and begin his new life in a new country.

They found old Humphrey lying in a drunken sleep on the damp floor of the hut, at the foot of the ladder, which he had not been able to climb up; and they had to drag him on one side to carry their burden to its resting-place in the loft overhead. He was an old man, with his brain softened and soddened with drink, and he could not be made to understand what had happened, or be persuaded to let Ishmael remain even for a few hours in his old home. It was only now and then, when his father was away during the few days that intervened before the funeral, that he could steal in to look at his mother's calm and placid face, from which the wrinkles, graved sharply on it by many troubles, seemed almost smoothed away. But every house in the parish was open to him—the castaway who had been driven from his home and thrown upon the world. He followed his mother to the grave, and stood for the last time amid his father and brothers. There was a whole crowd of villagers and neighbors gathered about the grave; and Nutkin was there with the little boy whom Ishmael had sought and found in the windings of the old quarry.

"I'd like to shake hands with all the Medways," said Nutkin, as the crowd began to melt away, "and let bygones be bygones. And, Ishmael, the squire bid me say, is there nothing as he can do for you, nothing as 'ud make it worth your while to stay at home, 'stead o' going to America?"

"Nothin'," answered Ishmael; "there's no home for me now mother's gone. It was home, sweet home, and I shall never have another."

But ten years after, when Ishmael came back to England, not to stay, but only to visit the old place, he had made a home for himself, with Elsie in it for his wife. He owned a farm of his own, and was prospering in every way. He found the old hut fallen into ruins; for his father had died in the workhouse the year after he had left England, and no one had lived in the desolate hovel since. The old door-sill was there yet, though the thatched roof had long ago moldered away; and he could almost fancy he saw his mother sitting there, and looking out for him.

The trees behind the ruins tossed their green branches in the wind, and the blue sky, flecked with clouds, shone above them, as in the bygone days. There were the old pleasant sounds, the song of the birds, and the hum of insects, and the rustling of myriads of leaves; but still it was no more home. His mother, who had made this poor hut a home for him, was no longer there.

"I remember," said Elsie softly, with her hand in his, "how she said, 'I shall watch for thee on the door-sill, to come into the Father's house, boldly, where He's gone to prepare a place; and you and me'll be at home again, with Him.'"

Made in United States
North Haven, CT
27 January 2024

47964980R00038